37 Jade Street
Walla Walla, WA 99362

The MONSTER DOG

❤ A Small Dog with a Big Heart ❤
Learns About Alzheimer's Disease

Written by Carmen Tribbett
Illustrated by Katie Hunerdosse

www.foxpointepublishing.com/author-carmen-tribbett
Promotion by Fox Pointe Publishing LLP

Library of Congress Cataloging-in-Publication Data
Tribbett, Carmen, author.
Hunerdosse, Katie, illustrator.
Farr, Chelsea, designer.
The Monster Dog; A Small Dog with a Big Heart Learns About
Alzheimer's Disease / Carmen Tribbett. - First edition.
Summary: A story about one family's experience with Alzheimer's
disease, written from the family dog's perspective.
ISBN 9780578571188 (hardcover)
1. Children's Fiction. 2. Illness. 3. Death & Dying. 4. Grief & Healing. 5. Pets.
Library of Congress Control Number: 2019913279

Printed and bound in the United States of America
First printing October 2019

A Note to Parents from the Author

This is a story of love and loss. It is hard to watch someone you love fade away from you. The forgetting is painful. It hurts to see the confusion and the closing off inside of someone you love.

Understanding dementia is often bewildering for adults but can be even more so for children. During the course of Ken's illness, I observed that sometimes children were scared, and became quiet and confused. Other children were filled with nervous energy. I sensed they did not understand what was happening to the person they loved, who was changing before their eyes.

People do not physically die from Alzheimer's disease. But with each day, a piece of that person seems to slip away. The person with Alzheimer's disease dies day-by-day.

Tasse and I hope her story of love and devotion will help children understand the hurts and joys of loving someone with Alzheimer's disease. Loving a person with Alzheimer's disease means accepting that they might forget you in their mind, but they will always remember you in their heart.

Dedicated to the men in my life:

Ken Tribbett,
who with graciousness and dignity,
accepted life with Alzheimer's disease;

Our son, John Tribbett,
who was always there with love, comfort,
and support for all those many years;

And Ken's greatly loved grandsons,
Scott and Jack Lessman,
with the hope they will remember
the happy days with Grandpa Ken.

Always remember, as Tasse says,
*"I know if he forgot me in his mind,
he will always remember me in his heart."*

Chapter 1
Happy Times
"It was love at first sight!"

The years have passed. I am much older now, but I remember it like it was yesterday. Let me tell you about it, for I loved him so.

I knew Ken was special when he walked into the room. He smiled, and his voice was soft. I could tell he was a kind and gentle man in every sense of the word.

He was a real Sweet Love.

Ken sat on the floor, and my brother quickly jumped in his lap. Ken laughed and patted my brother. I was beside myself; I wanted him to pet me! I stood on the other side of the room and wondered what to do. I decided to wag my tail and bark three times. "Woof! Woof! Woof!" I hoped he would notice me.

Carmen, Ken's wife, asked him, "Which puppy do you want?" I was so afraid and said to myself, *"Choose me! Choose me!"* Then he pointed to me and said, "That one!" They took me home. I was so happy, for I loved him so.

Now I had a family to love. There were Ken and Carmen, their children, Elizabeth and John, and their grandchildren, Scott and Jack.

From the very beginning, I was really Ken's dog. He named me Tasse. We were best friends! We did everything together. Ken had a sixty-year-old Oldsmobile coupe. We took the neighborhood kids and Ken's friends for rides in it. I loved it! I hung out the window and felt the wind blowing in my ears.

He taught me all kinds of tricks. I could shake hands and sit up. My favorite trick was to give three cheers for Augusta Community High School. I love to bark, so when he said, "Give me three cheers for Augusta Community High," I would bark three times! "Woof! Woof! Woof!" It was fun! It made Ken laugh. It made me so happy to hear him laugh.

One day at lunch, Ken rolled a tuna fish can across the floor as a joke. I grabbed it, and the tuna fish can became my favorite toy. I used to pick it up, growl, and throw it in the air. Then, I would pounce on it with my foot to keep it from rolling away. They called me the "Monster Dog" because I made so much noise. Ken would laugh and it made me happy, for I loved him so.

"I hung out the window
and felt the wind blowing in my ears."

We used to dog-sit Atman, a big dog belonging to Ken and Carmen's son, John. Atman and I looked funny together because I was so small and he was so big.

One day, Atman and I got in big trouble. Carmen had been preparing supper, and she left lamb chops on the counter when she answered the phone. It was all Atman's fault because he could easily reach them. You guessed it! We ate the lamb chops! Carmen and Ken had to eat tuna fish for supper. I thought to myself, *"I think I better leave my tuna fish can in the toy box tonight!"*

Atman was, as I said, a really big fellow. He had a yellow ball that he would bounce up and down. He would throw it up in the air, and then chase it. Sometimes his yellow ball would go over the fence. Atman would jump over the fence and then jump back into the yard with his ball. Ken decided to build a new fence so Atman and I would stay in the backyard. Even a new fence couldn't stop us, though!

Another day, Atman threw his ball, and it went over the new fence. He jumped over and then jumped back into the yard with his ball. I had to do something, so I crawled under the fence, just once, to prove that I could. Whew! It was a tight fit! Ken didn't see us, and he never knew. I didn't want to hurt his feelings!

4

"I crawled under the fence,
just once, to prove that I could."

Another day, when Ken and I were walking, we went by a house with a big dog barking at us from his front window. *"What fun!"* I thought. *"I will give him something to bark about!"*

I stopped and smelled his big tree. I smelled and smelled and smelled. He acted like he would break through the window because he was pawing and barking so fiercely. I, of course, ignored him and pretended I didn't hear him.

Then I scratched in his grass a couple of times. I didn't look up at the window, or to the right, or to the left. I just wagged my tail and sashayed on down the sidewalk. We could hear the big dog barking for quite a long time. Great fun!

Ken said, "Oh, Tasse, you are a Monster Dog, but I love you so!"

Chapter 2
Forgetting, Falling, and Fading

One day, I heard Carmen talking on the phone. She revealed Ken had Alzheimer's disease. I didn't know what that meant, but I would soon learn as he began to forget more and more.

Ken and I went for lots of walks. In fact, one day we went for too many! Ken forgot we had gone in the morning and afternoon and early evening — and so he wanted to go yet again! That was enough for me! *"Enough already!"* I thought. So I looked at Carmen as if to say, *"Do I really have to go again?"* She simply got my leash, patted me on the head, and off we went again. It was okay because I realized he didn't remember we had already gone three times that day. I thought to myself, *"Sometimes you just have to do things for people you love, even when you don't want to."*

When we go for a walk, it is my special time. I know how to heel, but I only do it when I want to. My leash is very long, so I can go way ahead to smell and investigate. It is a good thing because after a while, I realized Ken didn't recognize where we were or how to get home. I knew it was my job to lead Ken home. For a very long time, I don't think Carmen knew I was leading him home. Some dogs are seeing-eye dogs, but I had become a seeing-Ken-home dog.

Sometimes when I walked with Carmen, I was naughty; I might stop too long in one place to smell and smell and smell, or I might pull too far ahead. Over time, I began to sense I could no longer goof around that way with Ken. As his balance got worse and worse, I knew I had to slowly and gently lead him on our walks.

I heard Carmen tell her friend the Alzheimer's disease was worse, and now Ken had Parkinson's disease, too. She said that would make it even harder for Ken to balance and walk.

It was true. One day, Ken fell down and broke his glasses. He went to the emergency room and got stitches around his eye. After that, our walks became shorter, and Carmen came along with us.

8

The biggest change was Ken started to leave the house during the day to go to adult daycare.

At adult daycare, he made friends with other people who had Alzheimer's disease or other forms of dementia. Dementia means your brain has caused you to be mixed up sometimes and to forget more and more. People with dementia often remember things that happened a long time ago, and they often like to talk about those memories with other grownups or children. It is strange, though, because sometimes they can't remember what happened yesterday or even what they had for breakfast.

Ken and his new friends were at adult daycare for almost six hours each day, Monday through Friday, just like school. They shared stories, did crafts, exercised, and ate lunch together.

But the best part about adult daycare was that the driver and the aides came and picked him up in a big van. I liked that because I made new friends. They brought him home a little after three in the afternoon. I barked and barked when I heard the van coming. I waited at the door to greet him. I sometimes got in the way. The aides laughed because they knew I was so happy to see him. They could tell we were best friends and that I loved him so.

When he came home, he was always so tired. He would sit in his chair and quickly fall asleep. I slept, too, with my head on his foot. He was so very tired all the time. He started going to bed earlier and earlier. Finally, Carmen tucked us in every night at eight o'clock. I say "tucked us in," for I no longer slept in my little pink bed. I went to bed when he did and slept with my head on his knee. He liked that and so did I!

Ken became more and more tired. He became weaker and weaker. He fell more and more. I didn't know what to do. One Sunday, Carmen's brother came to visit. The next morning, he helped Ken down the steps and to the car. I realize now that this was the day Ken went to live at the care center. I waited at three o'clock for him to come home. But there was no van. I waited day after day for many days. But Ken didn't come home.

It broke my heart It must have broken Carmen's heart, too, because she was very sad.

Carmen was so tired and sad that I sat on her lap and tried to comfort her. We felt very sad for about a month. I didn't want to bark at the crow in our backyard, or tease the dog in the window, or go for walks, or eat treats, or anything. I just sat by the door every day at three o'clock, but Ken never came home again.

"I just sat by the door...
but Ken never came home again."

Chapter 3
Visiting Ken

Carmen took me to visit Ken. He was in the nursing home part of the care center be cause he needed so much help doing things like standing up and brushing his teeth.

After a while, I noticed when some dogs came to visit, they seemed scared. Maybe it was the strange smells, or the long halls, or the many people in wheelchairs. Of course, I was never scared, not even the first time!

Most of the people were glad to see me. I learned many older people just love children and dogs, so I made many new friends. They would pat my head and call me a "good dog." The best part was Ken was there at the end of the hall. That made me happy, for I loved him so.

I wasn't scared because I'm not scared of anything, except thunder. (Well, I guess everyone is scared of something.)

I'm so scared of thunder that I have a special thunder jacket I can wear and a special blanket to comfort me when it is thundering. I also carry and cuddle my toy bear when the thunder scares me. It is good to have something to comfort you. Sometimes, people with Alzheimer's disease find comfort in a special thing. Ken had a special quilt to keep him warm and comfy.

I loved to go to the care center to visit Ken. Carmen would be driving and, at first, I couldn't tell for sure where we were going. I would get too excited if Carmen told me before we left the house. If Carmen turned north on Fourth Street, I knew I'd be getting a bath and a haircut. I love when that happens, so I would yip all the rest of the way to the groomer's. But, if she turned *south* on Fourth Street, I soon figured out we were going to the care center to see Ken. Then, I would yip even louder all the rest of the way because I was even happier.

Once there, I knew the way to Ken's room. At first, I went yipping down the hall. Next to barking, I like yipping best of all; yipping is my special high-pitched bark. But I had to learn to be quieter. One day, Carmen and I had a nice visit with Ken. He patted my head and said, "My sweet Tasse!" He hadn't said my name in so long. It made me really happy.

I had many friends at the nursing home, so I went down the hall to see Abbie and some of my other friends.

When I came back to Ken's room, he said, "Oh look, a puppy!" *"A puppy?"* I thought. *"Did he forget? I'm almost twelve years old!"*

It made me sad and confused to think he might forget me, but I thought, *"I know if he forgot me in his mind, he will always remember me in his heart."*

We always brought Ken a "people treat" when we went to visit. He especially liked chocolate. We also brought dog treats for me. Carmen would give Ken a dog treat, and he would give it to me. Once, he must have been very confused because he started to put my dog treat in his mouth. He wanted to eat my dog treat instead of his chocolate! It made me sad to see him so confused, but I knew he couldn't help it.

One day, Ken's nurse called and left a message saying it was a really good day for Ken. We rushed out to see him. He remembered me that day! I was so happy. Carmen lifted me up to his lap, but I got too excited. I wanted to be so close that I tried to snuggle near his neck. Because I moved too quickly, I startled him, and I felt so sorry, for I loved him so. From then on, I remembered to move slowly so I wouldn't startle him. That worked better.

Ken had his eighty-fifth birthday soon after. We served his favorite, carrot cake, for his party. Everyone loves a party, and it was great fun! The nurses, staff, and many of his friends at the nursing home enjoyed the cake and sang "Happy Birthday" to him. I had a piece of cake, too, and wished him a happy birthday. It was a joyful time!

*"Everyone loves a party,
and it was great fun!"*

After that happy day, Ken became quieter and quieter. He slept more and more. When we would come to visit Ken, he would usually be in bed covered with his quilt that was so comforting to him. I would get up on the bed and put my head on his knee — just as we had done at home. It made me happy to be near him. I noticed that some grandmas and grandpas at the care center got crabby. Ken didn't. He just got quieter and quieter and drifted into his own world. He seemed so very far away.

It was hard. We never knew if it would be a good day and Ken would be happy to see us, or if he would be lost in his own thoughts. He seemed so empty inside. It often appeared as if he didn't know we were there. Sometimes, we just sat there and Carmen would hold his hand. One day, when we thought he didn't know we were there, he picked up her hand and kissed it. Another day, when she was reading the twenty-third Psalm to Ken, I noticed he folded his hands when she read, "though I walk through the valley of the shadow of death, I will fear no evil."

Sometimes, you can't know what a person with memory problems understands. "We just have to be there for him," Carmen said one day while driving home.

Not long after that, Carmen went to the nursing home and didn't come home all night. Carmen and their son, John, sat up all night with Ken and, early the next morning, he died. John brought all of Ken's things home – his books, his pictures, his clothes, his quilt... I sensed he would never be home again, and it made me sad. Carmen gave me Ken's old down jacket. It smelled just like him, and to this day, I snuggle in Ken's jacket. It makes me happy, for I loved him so.

Chapter 4
Happy Times Again

It hurts. It hurts when someone you love dies. Let me tell you what happened just the other day. When Ken was alive, he just loved to ride bicycles. Ken had many bicycles and was a great cyclist. I remember he rode his bike almost every day until he couldn't balance anymore. It was strange. I was sitting in the open doorway watching Carmen water flowers. Suddenly, I saw a man on a bike come down the road toward our house.

I was so excited because, just for a moment, I thought Ken was coming home! I ran out the door to greet him. I wagged and wagged my tail. I was so excited! But the man rode past our house and didn't come up our driveway. He kept on going, so I knew it wasn't Ken.

My heart sank and my tail dropped; I was so disappointed. I looked back once more, but there was no one there. I walked slowly into the house. I was so very sad. I miss him so.

It has now been more than a year since Ken left us and went to Heaven. We still miss seeing him, but now I am older. I have learned that life goes on. We are content. I often make Carmen laugh, and I like to play tricks on her. Actually, I am back to being the "Monster Dog" again!

One of my favorite tricks is to hide in one of my secret hiding places when she says, "Let's go outside." When she opens the door and looks down, I'm not there. I hear her say, "Where is that dog now?" I have hidden in one of my hiding places. She has to look for me. She has to come into the living room because she cannot see me from the patio door. Sometimes she laughs and says, "Oh Tasse, you are a Monster Dog, but I love you so!"

Other times when I get up, I stretch and stretch. I do a kind of slow ballet dance on my way to the door. I think Carmen prays for patience as she says, "Tasse, come!" or "Outdoors!" or "Outdoors now!" or "Tasse!" in a frustrated voice. I love the attention and when I get near the door, I run past her and wave my tail to and fro. She has to laugh! It is a fun way to start the day.

Another fun thing I like to do is at bedtime. I always bring a toy when I am tucked into my little pink bed at night. Sometimes, if I am not sleepy, I play with my toy. I talk to it, and I squeak it and squeak it and squeak it until Carmen says, "Enough, please. I can't sleep with all that noise. Go to sleep, Tasse!"

Other times, if the squeaker is broken, I throw the toy and run and find it, just like old times with the tuna can. The next morning, Carmen picks it up and says, "You must have had a bad night." But I didn't; I actually had a lot of fun!

Now that I am much older, I don't do some things I did as a puppy like chew furniture, but I still have good taste. I have discovered peanut butter! Carmen and I were having a little battle over some medicine that didn't taste good, so Carmen hid the pill in peanut butter. Well, now I love peanut butter even more than dog treats!

Now, I sit and look hungry and sad and I won't eat my dog food until she puts some peanut butter on it. One day, I had to look hungry and sad all day before she gave in and put peanut butter on my food. I am getting her trained!

"I throw the toy and run and find it!"

It has been more than a year since Ken left us and went to Heaven. We still miss being with him, but now that I am older, I realize it is part of God's plan to be born, live life, have our bodies die, and our spirits move on to Heaven.

Carmen says Ken was a good man. We try to remember his well-lived life. We try to remember happy times when he was strong and well. We are pleased he is no longer sick, or forgetful, or confused.

But best of all, she says that, someday, all three of us — Carmen, Ken, and I — will be together again in Heaven.

That makes me happy, for I loved him so.

"Someday... we'll all be together in Heaven."

*A love story about
a small Shih Tzu
and her person...*

Ken holding Tasse as a puppy

Narrated by Tasse Tribbett

Written by Carmen Tribbett

Carmen Tribbett taught sixth grade, was a registered nurse, and taught nursing skills at Riverland Community College. She lives in Austin, Minnesota, with the real "Monster Dog," who continues to be an inspiration for her writing.

Illustrated by Katie Hunerdosse

Katie Hunerdosse graduated from Luther College in 2008 with a degree in art. She lives in Austin, Minnesota, with her husband, two "monster dogs" of her own, and pursues artistic endeavors as frequently as her toddler son will allow.

CPSIA information can be obtained
at www.ICGtesting.com
Printed in the USA
LVHW012146101119
636862LV00015B/42/P

9 780578 571188